ANNA DEWDNEY & REED DUNCAN

ANIMALICIOUS

A Quirky ABC Book

illustrations by
CLAUDIA BOLDT

Penguin Workshop

The world is full of animals
of every single kind.
This book contains some special ones
that you won't often find.

You think you know your animals?
Here's some you've never seen—
some day you may encounter them
or see them in a dream.

Some are black and some are purple
and yellow, blue, and green.
Some are nice, some are funny,
and some are just plain mean.

ALLEYGATOR

ANONYMOUSE

BLABOON

BOA CONSTRUCTOR

COWABUNGA

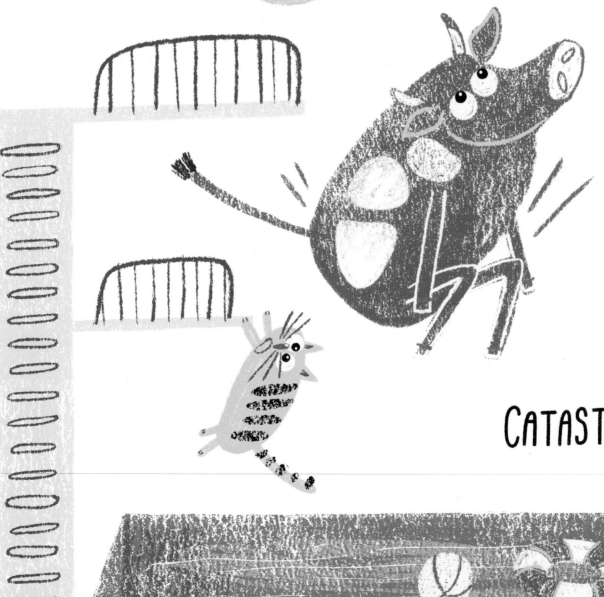

CATASTROPHE

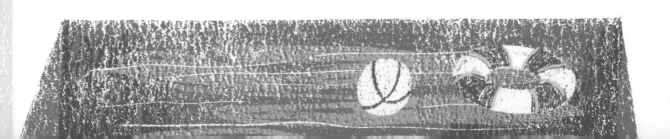

DUST BUNNY

DOODLEBUG

ELEPHANTOM

ELEGANT

FLATAPUS

FIREFLY

F

GRABBIT

GRRRILLA

HIPPOPOTAMESS

INCREDIBULL

IGNORANT

JOWL

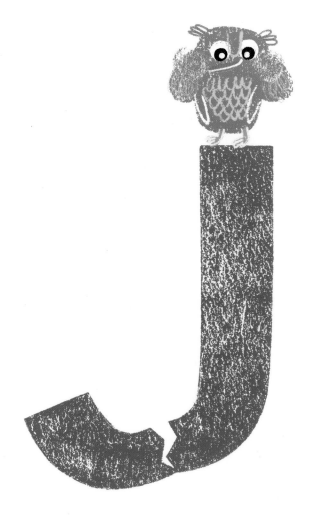

JYNX

KANGARUDE

KNOCKTOPUS

LIEON

LOBSTER

MACAWBRE

MASTIFF

MOUSETACHE

NEEWWWW!!T

NOCTURTLE

OSTRICH

PIETHON

POLAR BARE

PEARROT

QUAIL

QUARTER HORSE

RAINDEER

RHINOSAWRUS

R

ROCKTOPUS

SCAPEGOAT

STUMBLEBEE

SPYDER

SNORCA

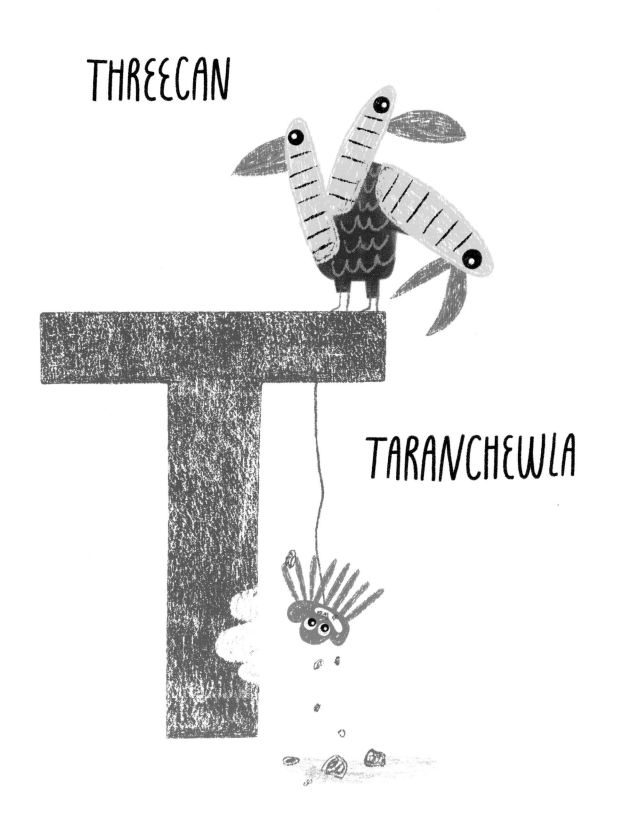

THREECAN

TARANCHEWLA

UNSTABULL

UNICORN

VANATEE

VAMOOSE

WHEREWOLF

WEESEL

WALRUSH

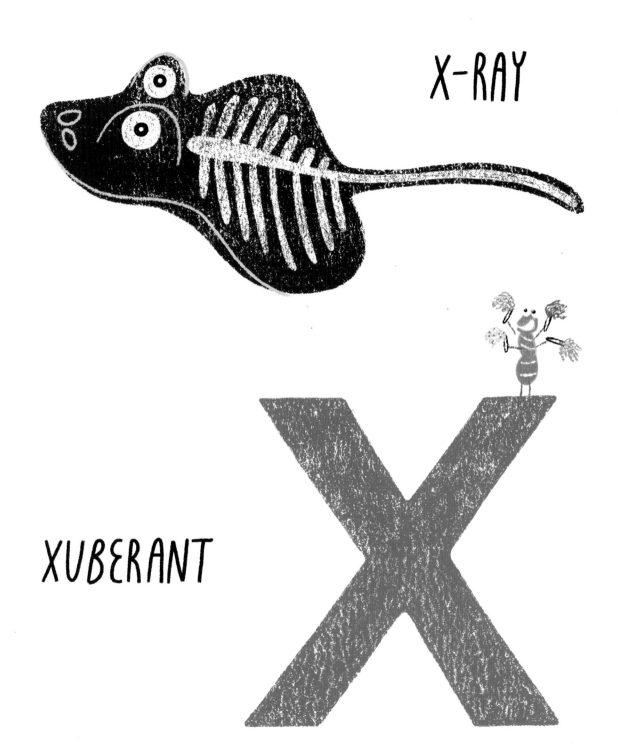

X-RAY

XUBERANT

YEARLING

YOWL

YAK YAK YAK

ZEBRAWN

ZIPPIRANHA

So now you've met these animals.
They're quite a funny crew!
We think they're really out there somewhere;
more importantly—do you?